Five reasons why we think you'll love this book!

Winnie AND Wilbur
WINNIE THE WITCH

The story is full of slapstick moments.

This is your chance to see inside Winnie's bathroom!

There is so much to spot in every picture.

You can take the Winnie and Wilbur challenge:

Wilbur a   re.

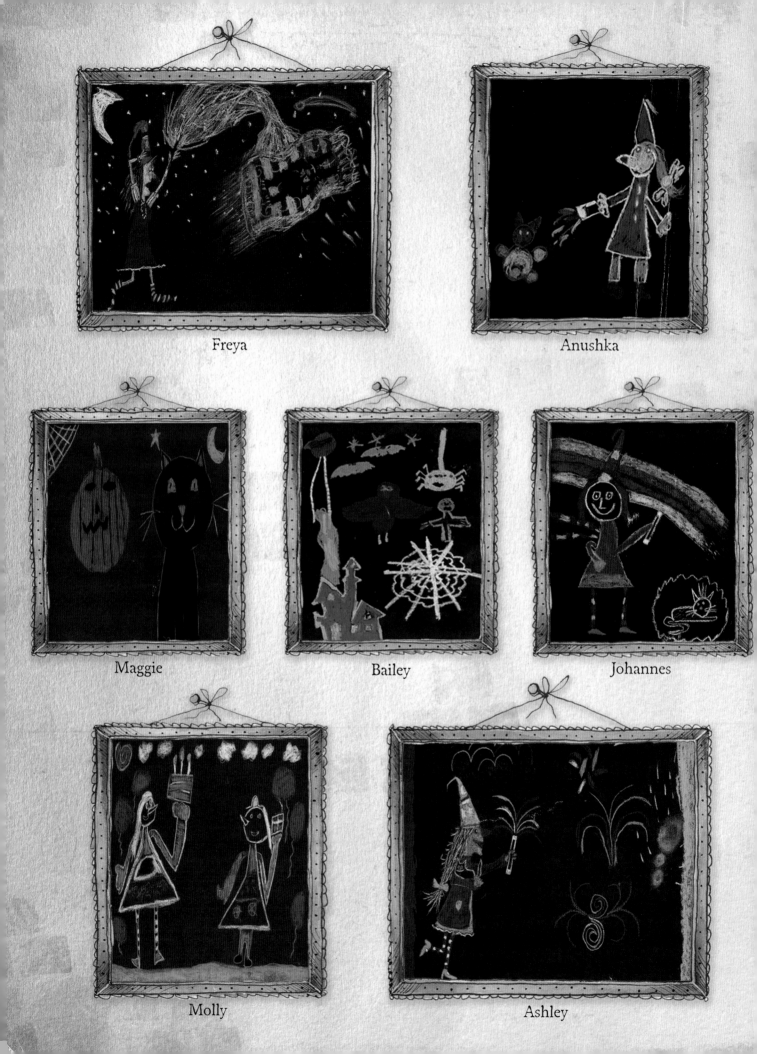

Freya

Anushka

Maggie

Bailey

Johannes

Molly

Ashley

Amber

Jun-Yeong

Pablo

Matilda

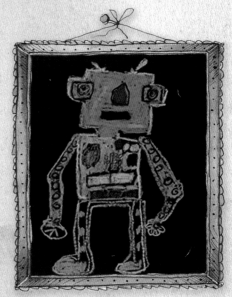

Marwin

Hasan

Rebecca

Thank you to all these schools for helping with the endpapers:

St Barnabas Primary School, Oxford; St Ebbe's Primary School, Oxford; Marcham Primary School, Abingdon; St Michael's C.E. Aided Primary School, Oxford; St Bede's RC Primary School, Jarrow; The Western Academy, Beijing, China; John King School, Pinxton; Neston Primary School, Neston; Star of the Sea RC Primary School, Whitley Bay; José Jorge Letria Primary School, Cascais, Portugal; Dunmore Primary School, Abingdon; Özel Bahçeşehir İlköğretim Okulu, Istanbul, Turkey; the International School of Amsterdam, the Netherlands; Princethorpe Infant School, Birmingham.

OXFORD
UNIVERSITY PRESS

Great Clarendon Street, Oxford OX2 6DP

Oxford University Press is a department of the University of Oxford. It furthers the University's objective of excellence in research, scholarship,and education by publishing worldwide. Oxford is a registered trade mark of Oxford University Press in the UK and in certain other countries

British Library Cataloguing in Publication Data available

ISBN: 978-0-19-274816-4 (paperback)
ISBN: 978-0-19-274905-5 (paperback and CD)

10 9 8 7 6 5 4 3 2 1

Printed in China

Paper used in the production of this book is a natural, recyclable product made from wood grown in sustainable forests. The manufacturing process conforms to the environmental regulations of the country of origin

www.winnieandwilbur.com

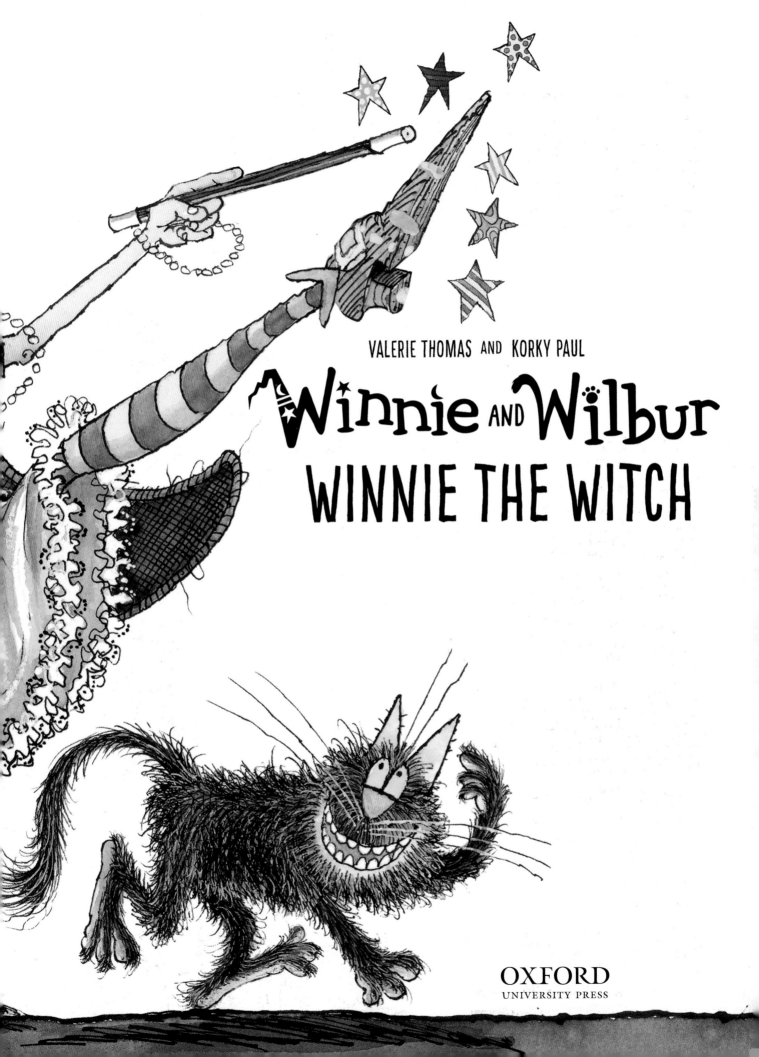

VALERIE THOMAS AND KORKY PAUL

Winnie and Wilbur
WINNIE THE WITCH

OXFORD
UNIVERSITY PRESS

Winnie the Witch lived in a
black house in the forest.
The house was black on the
outside and black on the inside.
The carpets were black.
The chairs were black.
The bed was black and it had
black sheets and black blankets.
Even the bath was black.

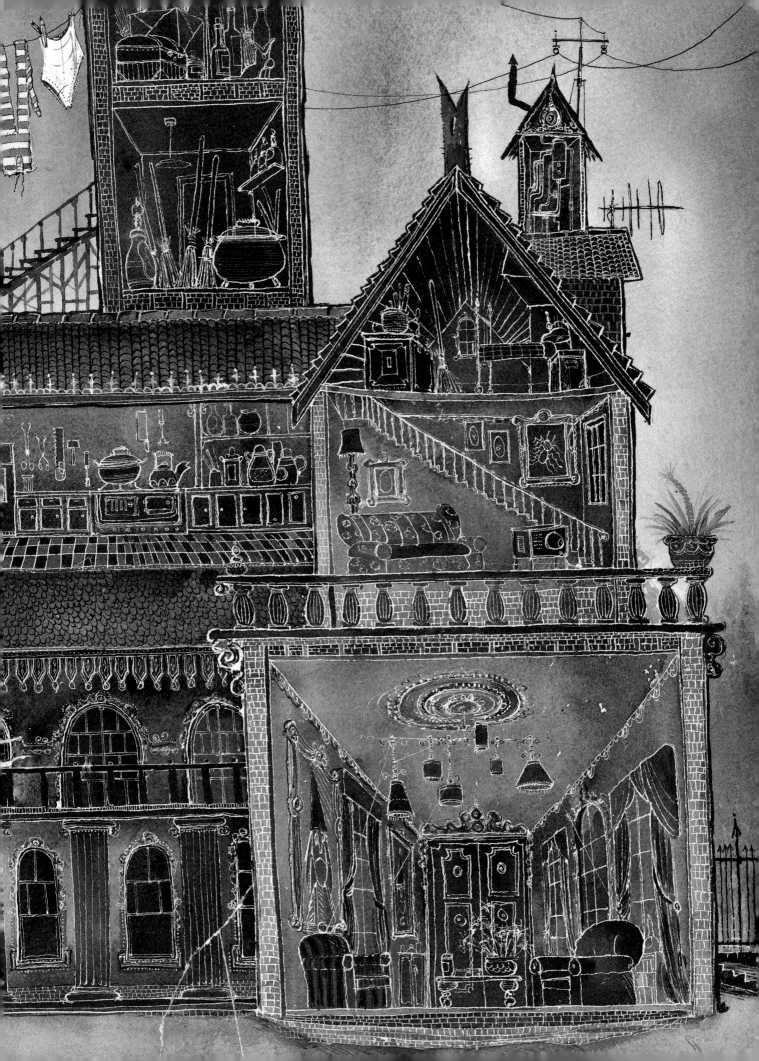

Winnie lived in her black house with her cat, Wilbur.
He was black too. And that is how the trouble began.

When Wilbur sat on a chair with
his eyes open, Winnie could see him.
She could see his eyes, anyway.

But when Wilbur closed his eyes
and went to sleep, Winnie couldn't
see him at all. So she sat on him.

When Wilbur sat on the carpet with
his eyes open, Winnie could see him.
She could see his eyes, anyway.

But when Wilbur closed his
eyes and went to sleep,
Winnie couldn't see him at all.
So she tripped over him.

One day, after a nasty fall, Winnie decided something had to be done. She picked up her magic wand, waved it once and **Abracadabra!** Wilbur was a black cat no longer. He was bright green!

'Abracadabra!'

Now, when Wilbur slept on a chair, Winnie could see him.

When Wilbur slept on the floor, Winnie could see him.

And she could see him
when he slept on the bed.
But, Wilbur was not allowed
to sleep on the bed . . .

. . . so Winnie put
him outside.
Outside in
the grass.

Winnie came hurrying outside,
tripped over Wilbur,
turned three somersaults,
and fell into a rose bush.

When Wilbur sat outside in the grass,
Winnie couldn't see him, even when
his eyes were wide open.

This time, Winnie was furious.
She picked up her magic wand,
waved it five times and . . .

. . . Abracadabra! Wilbur had a red head,
a yellow body, a pink tail, blue whiskers,
and four purple legs.
But his eyes were still green.

Now, Winnie could see Wilbur when
he sat on a chair, when he lay on the
carpet, when he crawled into the grass.

And even when
he climbed
to the top
of the
tallest
tree.

Wilbur climbed to the top of the tallest tree to hide.
He looked ridiculous and he knew it.
Even the birds laughed at him.

Wilbur was miserable.
He stayed at the top
of the tree all day
and all night.

Next morning Wilbur
was still up the tree.
Winnie was worried.
She loved Wilbur
and hated him to
be miserable.

Then Winnie had an idea.
She waved her magic wand
and **Abracadabra!**
Wilbur was a black cat once more.
He came down from the tree, purring.

Then Winnie waved her wand again, and again, and again.

'Abracadabra!'

Now instead of a black house,
she had a yellow house with a
red roof and a red door.
The chairs were white with red
and white cushions. The carpet
was green with pink roses.

The bed was blue, with pink and white sheets and pink blankets. The bath was a gleaming white.

And now, Winnie can see Wilbur no matter where he sits.

Bethany

Katia

Eun-Jae

Kathleen

Ji-Eun

Jenny

Sara

Fraser

Ka Keung

Selin

Olivia

Siyabend

Kieran

A note for grown-ups

Oxford Owl is a FREE and easy-to-use website packed with support and advice about everything to do with reading.

Informative videos

Hints, tips and fun activities

Top tips from top writers for reading with your child

Help with choosing picture books

For this expert advice and much, much more about how children learn to read and how to keep them reading ...

LOOK
for Oxford Owl
www.oxfordowl.co.uk